FEAR YOUR ENEMY

THOMAS FINCHAM

Fear Your Enemy
Thomas Fincham

AUTHOR'S NOTE
This book is a work of fiction. Names, characters, places and incidents are products of the author's imagination or are used fictitiously. Any resemblance to actual events or locales or persons, living or dead, is entirely coincidental.

The scanning, uploading and distribution of this book via the internet or any other means without the permission of the publisher is illegal and punishable by law. Please purchase only authorized electronic editions, and do not participate in or encourage electronic piracy of copyrighted materials. Your support of the author's rights is appreciated.

Visit the author's website:
www.finchambooks.com

Contact:
finchambooks@gmail.com

Join my Facebook page:
https://www.facebook.com/finchambooks/

MARTIN RHODES

1) Close Your Eyes
2) Cross Your Heart
3) Say Your Prayers
4) Fear Your Enemy

ONE

He stood outside the front door but did not ring the doorbell. It was a two-story house with a brown brick exterior and a triangular roof. It had a two-car garage with a wide walkway leading up to the entrance. The lawn was recently mowed, and a flower bed encircled the green grass.

Martin Rhodes did not care for any of it.

Rhodes was slim with salt-and-pepper hair. He was clean-shaven, and he stood over six-foot-four. He had on a long coat that hung over his broad shoulders. He carried a duffel bag that contained all his belongings.

His deep blue eyes were transfixed by the buzzer, but he did not dare push it.

He wasn't sure why he was there, but he knew it had to be important, or why else would he have received the call?

Since leaving the city of Franklin, he had not had any contact with anyone, except for his best friend, Detective Tom Nolan.

Rhodes didn't own a cell phone, but every once in a while, he would use a pay phone to get in touch with Nolan. Rhodes was in an obscure, industrial town in search of a job when he had contacted Nolan.

What Nolan told him made him drop everything and head straight for Parish, a quiet town on the East Coast.

Rhodes was debating whether he should turn back when the door swung open.

"Martin, I'm so happy to see you," said Angela Fulton, formerly Angela Rhodes.

She was much smaller than her ex-husband, standing slightly over five-foot-two. She was slim but had packed on a few pounds over the years. She had curly blonde hair, and unlike Rhodes, she had bright green eyes.

When people would see them together, they couldn't understand how Martin and Angie had ever got married. He was big and rough-hewn while she was small and refined.

But he knew why he had married her. She made him feel both strong and weak. He could do anything with her next to him, but without her, he was nothing.

When she had informed him she wanted a divorce, it was the second-worst day of his life. The first was when the judge gave him life in prison for first-degree murder.

"Angie…" he said, but then he stopped. Angie was his nickname for her, but now that they were no longer a couple, he wasn't sure if it was appropriate or not.

She smiled. "It's been a long time since anyone's called me by that name. Come in." He entered. She led him to the living room. "I knew you were coming, so I sent the kids to Harold's mom's house."

Rhodes was aware that she had remarried and that she had two young children. Rhodes was also aware that her husband, Harold Fulton, was a pharmacist with his own dispensary in the town of Parish.

"Can I get you something to drink?" she asked.

"No, I'm fine. Thank you," he said, taking a seat.

Angie sat across from him. He tried to look at the interior of the room, but his eyes kept falling back on her. He had always thought she was beautiful, and now, even though she was no longer his wife, he still felt that way.

He rubbed his big, sweaty palms on his jeans. He didn't know why he was so nervous.

"You look good," she said. "I see you've lost some weight."

Prior to going to prison, Rhodes was heavy and in terrible shape. But being stuck in a cell twenty-three hours a day gave him an opportunity to work on his body. Plus, he didn't have any other choice. As a former homicide detective, he had a large target on his back. The other inmates were more than willing to inflict their hatred for the police on him. Fortunately for Rhodes, he was big and strong and was able to defend himself. Toward the end of his sentence, no one messed with him anymore.

"I work out now," he finally said.

"And I see you shaved off that beard."

Rhodes rubbed his smooth cheek. "I know you used to like it."

"I never said I liked it," she replied with a laugh. "I just said I didn't mind it."

"I didn't know. I would have shaved it back then."

"When you're in love, you don't focus on trivial things like that."

Silence fell between them, which was to be expected. They had been apart for ten years. "I read the article on you in the *Daily Times*," Angie finally said. "That's how I knew you were released and living in Franklin."

7

Rhodes nodded. He had given Nolan's friend, Hyder Ali, an exclusive interview prior to leaving Franklin. Rhodes had two conditions for the interview, though. One: Ali didn't ask about the night he committed the murder. Two: Ali only printed the article once Rhodes had left Franklin.

Rhodes still hadn't read it, and he had no intention of doing so. But now that Angie had mentioned it, he wished he had at least given it a cursory look.

He was sure Ali hadn't said anything negative about him. Rhodes had, after all, helped capture the Franklin Strangler, a serial killer who had terrorized the citizens of Franklin. Plus, Nolan trusted Ali, and Rhodes saw no reason not to trust him either, or else he wouldn't have agreed to the interview in the first place.

Rhodes didn't care for the notoriety that he got as a convicted police detective. As far as he was concerned, he wanted his past to stay in the past. But he was mature enough to know it would not be easy.

"When I found out you were in Franklin," Angie said, "I knew you would be staying with Tom."

Technically, Nolan was on vacation when Rhodes had been released, but Rhodes did stay at Nolan's house during his time in Franklin.

"So I called Tom and told him I needed to speak to you," Angie continued. "Nolan told me you didn't have a number but that he would pass on my message the next time he spoke to you. I just wish it was sooner."

"Why? What's wrong?" Rhodes asked, sensing the trepidation in her voice.

She looked down at her hands and began to rub the wedding ring on her finger.

"Angie, tell me? What's going on?" he asked, concerned.

"I don't know how to say this…" Her words trailed off.

"You can tell me," he said.

She then looked him directly in the eyes. "Martin, my husband has been charged with murder."

TWO

Rhodes wasn't sure if he heard Angie correctly. "What did you say?"

"Harold is in jail. They think he murdered someone."

Rhodes fell back in his chair. He knew there was a reason why Angie had wanted to speak to him. He hoped it was to talk about what had happened between them. He never expected it would be this.

"Um…" he stammered, not sure where to begin. "Where… where is Harold now?"

"In the county jail," she replied.

"When did this happen?"

"Two weeks ago. It's also how long I've been trying to contact you."

Rhodes could only nod. Until he had spoken with Nolan, he had thought Angie wanted nothing to do with him. In fact, Rhodes wasn't even going to call Nolan that day. Now he was glad he did.

"What about bail?"

"The judge set it at one million dollars."

Rhodes was shocked. "Why one million?"

Angie sighed. "The prosecution convinced the judge that because Harold is a pharmacist, he has the resources to flee the country."

"Do you have the money?"

"We're comfortable, but we do not have anything near the one million they are asking for."

"What about Harold's parents? You said the children are with them right now. Can't they help out?"

"Harold's dad died when he was young, and his mom lives on a small pension. She has offered to sell the house Harold grew up in, but it still won't be enough. I would gladly sell this place, but we've got a big mortgage on it. Plus, Harold took out a bank loan to buy the pharmacy. He used to work for the previous owner, and when the owner decided to retire and sell it, Harold bought the place."

"Who's the victim?"

"His name is Kevin Williams."

"How does Harold know him?"

"He didn't really. Kevin Williams was homeless and an addict. Harold had caught him a few times stealing over-the-counter medication from the pharmacy. He would report him, and the police would take him away, but a few days later, Williams would be back on the street. Harold didn't make a big deal out of it. People are always shoplifting items here and there. But then the robberies started happening. They always happened at night. We have security cameras, but someone always managed to disable them."

"What did they take?" Rhodes asked.

"The more expensive drugs, ones only people with insurance can afford."

"And Harold was able to link those robberies to Williams?"

"Well, not exactly."

Rhodes was confused.

Angie said, "With the security cameras not functioning, we couldn't tell who had committed the break-ins. It wasn't until Harold received a call that something happened."

Rhodes sat up straight.

11

"It came in the middle of the night. I remember it because I was sleeping and only woke up when I heard Harold getting dressed. I asked where he was going, and he said to get his stuff back. I didn't know what he was talking about. I was half-asleep. But a few hours later, Harold woke me up again and told me something bad had happened. He was pale and shivering. I asked what had happened. Before he could tell me, the police were at our door."

She put her face in her hands.

Rhodes feared she would break down. He had seen her like this before. He had to keep her talking. Nothing was making sense right now.

"Who was the caller?" he asked.

"We don't know."

"What?"

"Harold didn't recognize the voice. It sounded like the caller had cupped the receiver to hide his identity."

"What about the number?"

"It was blocked."

"What did the caller say?"

"The caller told Harold that his stuff was at a crack house about an hour away from here."

"Why didn't Harold call the police?"

"The caller warned him that if he called the police, they might scare the robber away. The caller wanted Harold to come alone."

"Why?" Rhodes was suspicious.

"The caller wanted Harold to bring one thousand dollars in exchange for the information. Harold thought it was another addict on the line. They are always desperate for money, so he agreed."

"But things didn't turn out that way, did they?" Rhodes said.

"No, they didn't," she replied. "When Harold showed up at the address, he didn't find anyone waiting for him. Instead, he found the front door of the crack house open. He went in, and that's when he…"

She paused.

"He *what*, Angie?"

Her shoulders sagged. "I don't know the rest. Harold won't tell me the details. All I know is that inside that crack house, they found Kevin Williams's body. He had been shot. The police were able to match the bullet from the scene to a gun registered to Harold." Tears began to form in her eyes. "They also found bloodstains on Harold's coat, which they matched to Williams. The police believe Harold went to the house and shot and killed Williams to get his merchandise back."

She finally broke down.

Rhodes wanted to reach over and hold her. He wanted to console her like he did when they were married. But they weren't husband and wife anymore. He was a guest in her house.

She looked down at her feet. "I'm sorry… it's just been so difficult for me… I… I just can't believe it's happening again…"

Rhodes fully understood what she meant. Another husband of hers was going to prison for murder.

Rhodes leaned over and lifted her chin up so that she was facing him. "What I did, shooting that man, everybody saw it. I was guilty. I have never denied it. Angie, do you believe Harold did it?"

"I don't know," she replied. "I don't know anything anymore."

"Then, why did you call me?"

"I…" Angie sighed. "I want you to help Harold. You were a great detective—it was what made you shoot that person that night. You knew that man was guilty, and you couldn't see him get away with murder. If anyone can find out the truth, you can."

"What if I find Harold is guilty? Then what?"

Her shoulders sagged even more. "Then I'll start my life again, like before. But this time, I'll have my children to help me move on."

THREE

The office of Matheson, Rosenthal and Geltoff, LLP, was on the twentieth floor of a commercial building. It was neither spacious nor small. There was a secretary at the front desk with one overworked assistant in the back who handled all the clerical duties for the two lawyers, Rob Matheson and Isaac Rosenthal. Their partner, Jacob Geltoff, had retired two years ago. The remaining partners didn't bother removing his name. The costs would have been too much from changing signs and letterheads, not to mention all the print and television ads they were constantly running. Plus, having three names made their firm look bigger and more prestigious.

Rhodes and Angie were sitting in Rob Matheson's office. To say he was overweight would be an understatement. Matheson looked like a walrus dressed in a suit. His triple chin wiggled whenever he talked, his shirt buttons strained to hold his gut in, and a heavy mustache covered his small oval mouth.

"You were a detective?" he asked, examining Rhodes with his beady eyes.

"Yes, and I was charged and convicted for murder, which I served ten years in a federal penitentiary for." Rhodes wanted to get it out of the way before Matheson started cross-examining him. Lawyers, by nature, had a way of pushing and prodding until they got the answer they were looking for. Rhodes didn't want nor cared enough to hide his past. Sooner or later, Matheson would find out who he was and what he had done. Better he knew now than at the time when the prosecution started drilling into Rhodes's involvement in the case. He didn't want to become a stain on their defense if and when Harold went to trial.

"Right," Matheson said. "And you were married to Mrs. Fulton, is that correct?"

"Yes."

Matheson exhaled. "And now you are here to help exonerate Harold Fulton?"

"No."

Matheson was surprised.

"I'm here to find out the truth. If Harold Fulton is guilty, I'll leave you to defend him as you would any other client in his position. I will, however, help you find all the missing pieces, if there are any to be found, that could assist you in your case."

"So, you'll be like a private detective, but you'll work for us?"

Rhodes hadn't thought of it like that. "Yes."

Matheson leaned back in his chair and placed a fat palm over a file in front of him. "This is highly unusual. Whatever is in this file is strictly protected by the attorney-client privilege. We would prefer not to share anything pertinent to the case with an outsider, even if that outsider was somehow related to the client." He glanced over at Angie.

Angie said, "Harold is fully aware that I've called Martin. He wasn't in favor of it initially, but he knows the situation doesn't look good for him right now. If you need his consent regarding Martin, he will give it to you."

Matheson thought about it. "You are right. Mr. Fulton's case is highly one-sided right now. And I mean for the prosecution. The evidence is stacked up against him, I'm afraid. But that doesn't mean we won't fight for him."

Rhodes knew the lawyer was stating the obvious, or else what would be the point of hiring him in the first place? He would make the family believe that there was a possibility for acquittal, even if there was none, just so he could continue billing them.

Rhodes said, "Just let me see what you have on the case. The police report, Harold's statement, any witnesses. The more I know, the more I can work with."

The lawyer didn't look convinced.

"I trust Martin, and so does Harold," Angie added. "You can too."

Matheson looked over at a shelf filled with binders, folders, and boxes. They were filled with information on all the cases the firm was currently working on.

Matheson sighed and pushed the file across to Rhodes. "I'll say you are assisting me with the case. This will give you access to Mr. Fulton whenever you need it. It will also let you question anyone regarding the case. But if there are any irregularities or actions on your part that could impact the case or the reputation of this firm, you will be solely responsible for it."

"Agreed," Rhodes said.

"Also, I won't pay you. This is on your own dime," Matheson added. "I'm only agreeing to this because I'm up to my neck in pending cases, and right now, Mr. Fulton could use all the help he can get."

FOUR

Rhodes unlocked the door with a key that was attached to a large plastic fish. The motel was ocean-themed. The establishment may have once been a tourist attraction, but now, after years of neglect, the place looked like an environmental disaster.

The blue walls painted to resemble the sea were now an ugly green. The smiling, healthy mermaids now looked like diseased zombie-fish. The bright yellow that once invoked a feeling of energy and excitement now invoked a feeling of sickness and lassitude. Rhodes would normally never consider staying at such a place, but at fifty dollars a night, he couldn't complain.

Angie had offered to let him stay in her guest room, but he declined. Rhodes wasn't ready to be under the same roof as his ex-wife. Plus, he wasn't sure how her children would feel seeing a stranger in their house. It was bad enough that their father was not at home, but to see another man eating and sleeping there would send the wrong message.

Maybe he was overthinking it. Children were very resilient, and he was sure Angie would come up with a reason for why he was there, but that still wouldn't make him feel any more comfortable. In fact, he still wasn't sure how he felt when he was around her.

During the drive to the motel, the smell of Angie's perfume flooded his mind with memories of their time together. When he would lie in bed and stare at her sleeping, thinking how lucky he had been to be with her. Or when he would return to an empty house where her lingering smell would reassure him that she would be home soon.

Those times were gone, he knew. Things were more complicated now. Her family was on the brink of destruction, and she had asked him of all people to make sure that didn't happen.

He feared that being in close proximity to her could make him do something he would end up regretting.

No distractions, he told himself. *Not now. Not when I have to see the facts and the evidence objectively.*

He pushed the door open and entered the room.

He flicked the lights on and found himself staring at a space that was far too small for a man his size. There was a single bed with a side table next to it. Across was a cabinet with an old nineteen-inch television resting on top of it.

Rhodes walked over to it and pressed a button. The screen flickered as if it was being revived after a coma. Fortunately, a color image came on the television.

Rhodes moved to the bed and dropped his duffel bag on it.

He then proceeded to the bathroom. The sink and tub were rusted and stained. He turned on the tap and watched the water flow freely. He only shut it when he felt hot water in his palms.

He left the bathroom and sat on the bed. He could feel the coils underneath the mattress, but otherwise, the bed was manageable.

Rhodes couldn't really complain. The room was an upgrade from the cell he had spent ten years of his life in. The mattress in his cell had smelled of sweat and urine, and it felt like he was lying on a piece of wood. The toilet hardly ever flushed, and the taps only gave out chilly water. Plus, he had to share a shower with fifty other men, many of whom wouldn't hesitate to slice his throat open.

He placed his head on the pillow and let his feet hang over the side. The bed was short for his height, but again, he didn't grumble.

He was a free man, and that was the only thing that truly mattered to him.

FIVE

The guard gave Rhodes a once over and then examined the piece of paper in his hand.

Rhodes didn't have a suit or any other formal clothing, so he didn't fit the profile of an assistant at Matheson, Rosenthal and Geltoff, LLP.

Rhodes was at the county jail, hoping to get a meeting with Harold Fulton. The document in the guard's possession gave Rhodes authority to communicate with the accused on behalf of his attorney, Rob Matheson.

The guard finally nodded to a door and said, "Go through there."

After passing through a metal detector and entering his name in a visitor's logbook, Rhodes was escorted down the hall by another guard. Whenever the guard opened and shut a secure door, it reminded Rhodes of his time in prison. It was surprising how even the turning of a bolt or clicking of a lock could trigger memories of his sentence.

Rhodes clenched his jaw and kept in step next to the guard.

They stopped at a metal door with a small window. The guard unlocked it with a key and held the door for Rhodes. "Knock when you are done, and I'll come and get you."

Rhodes nodded and went in.

When the guard shut the door and locked it, Rhodes felt his heart sink to the bottom of his stomach. He took a deep breath and closed his eyes.

He didn't realize how powerful the impact of being back inside a cell again would be. The sights and smells of the jail made him feel claustrophobic. He had the urge to call the guard back and get the hell out of there.

"Are you okay?" he heard a voice say.

Rhodes opened his eyes and found a man staring at him. Harold Fulton was short and slim with prematurely graying hair. He had on a dress shirt, dress pants, and dress shoes. He wore a sleeveless sweater over the shirt.

He pushed his glasses up his thin nose and said, "I'm Harold."

They shook hands. The accused man's grip was firm, but his hand was cold.

"Please, have a seat," Harold said, offering his bed to Rhodes. He quickly sat on a stool that was next to a small table.

Rhodes took the hard mattress.

"Thank you for coming. I really appreciate it," Harold said. "Before we begin, I would like to clarify something."

Rhodes waited for him.

"I didn't know you were in prison when I met Angela. To be honest with you, I didn't even know she was married."

Rhodes believed him. He knew having a husband locked up for murder wasn't something anyone would mention on a first date.

"When I found out, we were already in love. By then, I didn't care. I just wanted to be with her and make her happy." He gave Rhodes a contrite look. "I'm sorry."

"Don't be," Rhodes replied. "It was my actions that destroyed our marriage, not you. I'm glad she's moved on."

Rhodes meant every word, no matter how hard it was to say them. Had he not done what he did, he believed Angie would still be married to him, and Harold would not have been in her life. But Rhodes's actions had left Angie in turmoil, and fortunately for her, Harold was there to bring her the calm and stability that she truly deserved.

"What happened on that night?" Rhodes finally asked.

Harold took a deep breath. "I'm not sure how much Angela has told you."

"She told me about the robberies and the call you received in the middle of the night. Tell me about the crack house specifically."

Harold exhaled. "Okay. When I got to the house, I waited for the person who had called me. I was supposed to pay him for information regarding the stolen merchandise from the pharmacy."

"Did you stop at a bank or ATM to withdraw the money?" Rhodes asked.

"No. I had cash from the pharmacy's sales for the day."

Rhodes frowned. He was hoping there was proof to confirm Harold's reasons for being at the crack house. "Go on."

"When the caller didn't show up, I decided to check out the house for myself."

"Why?"

"The front door was open."

"Someone had left it open?"

"I don't know, but I thought maybe the caller was waiting inside for me."

"Then what happened?"

"I went in. The place was in terrible condition. It smelled, and there was garbage and junk everywhere. It was disgusting."

That's what a crack house looks like, Rhodes thought.

"I went through each room in the house until I got to the second floor. In one of the rooms, I saw someone on the floor. It was dark and I thought they were sleeping. I said, hello. I knocked on the door. I even tried the light switches, but I guess there was no electricity. I got closer, and that's when I saw him. I knew who he was. Kevin Williams. I had caught him stealing small items from the store before, but I never imagined he would be the robber. I was about to wake him when I noticed a hole in his forehead. It looked like it was burnt. I was confused, and that's when I saw the pool of blood underneath his head." Harold shut his eyes and rubbed his temples. A pained expression came over his face.

"What did you do next?" Rhodes asked.

"I was terrified at what I had just seen. I ran out of the house and drove straight home."

"You didn't call 9-1-1?"

"I know I should have, but I knew how it would look if they caught me at the house."

"That you killed him?"

"Yes, but I didn't. I swear."

Rhodes could not tell whether Harold was lying or telling the truth. He was perfectly poker-faced.

"What about the gun?" Rhodes asked.

"What about it?"

"They found it in your vehicle. They matched it to the bullet recovered from Williams's body."

"That's the thing," Harold said. "I never took the gun with me. Why would I? If I knew something like this would happen, I would've never gone to that house. I thought some robber was trying to extort money out of me. I never thought there would be a murder."

"You say you didn't take the gun with you, but it was in the glove compartment of your car. The prosecution will say you shot Williams and were going to dispose of the murder weapon at a later time."

"I know how this looks," he said, raising his voice, but then he quickly lowered it. "I'm telling you, I never took the gun with me because I only keep it at the pharmacy."

Rhodes gave him a skeptical look. Harold sighed. "I bought the gun in case someone tried to rob the store. It was only for protection. My life wasn't in danger, so there was no need for me to carry it that night."

"Regardless, it was registered to you."

Harold's hands fell to his sides. "I know."

"Have you ever owned a gun before?" Rhodes asked.

Harold shook his head. "I'd never even held a gun before I got this one."

Rhodes paused for a moment, considering his next question. "What about the blood found on your coat and your car seat? How do you explain that?"

"It must have gotten on the coat when I knelt down to check the body. And when I drove away, it must have transferred from the coat to the car seat."

"What about the stolen items? Did you find them at the house?"

"Yes, they were next to the body."

"Did you take them?"

"No, I left them. I wanted to get away from there as fast as I could."

"Did anyone see you leave the house?"

"I don't know. It was all a blur."

Rhodes was quiet for a moment. He then asked, "Is there anything else you can tell me that can confirm what you are saying?"

"I've told you everything, and it's the truth."

Rhodes looked at Harold for a moment before he stood up to leave. "Are you going to help me?" Harold asked.

"I will, only because Angie asked me to. But I will tell you something: right now, if a jury heard what I just heard, they will—without a doubt— convict you of murder."

SIX

Rhodes needed a drink.

He found a bar not far from the county jail. He ordered a glass of bourbon and then found a table in the corner.

After a couple of sips, his nerves calmed down.

Rhodes was never great at keeping his emotions in check. It was what made him commit the crime that got him locked up. If he hadn't taken the case so personally, his life might have been different. For one thing, he wouldn't be living out of a motel, that's for sure. He wouldn't be struggling financially, as he would have still been employed as a detective. But more importantly, he wouldn't be alone.

He had no family, no money, and no home.

Rhodes emptied the glass and then ordered another. He felt a splitting headache coming on.

What made matters worse was that he didn't know what lay ahead for him. Where would he go? What would he do?

He couldn't stay in Parish. It was a small town, and news of his past would become public knowledge very soon. This would make acquiring gainful employment all that much more difficult.

Then there was the matter of his ex-wife. It was foolish of him to think he didn't have any feelings for her. He did.

Their divorce didn't occur because they were no longer in love. In fact, they were deeply committed to each other right up until his sentencing. Their marriage ended because he was inside and she was outside.

He couldn't blame her for moving on. She never asked much from him, and now he realized he didn't give her much in return.

His job was his main priority, and she had dutifully supported him. She believed that what he was doing was right. She tolerated his moody behavior. She accepted his long hours at work. The only thing she truly cared about was that he was loyal to her.

He was.

He never once strayed from their marriage. There were other women who had shown interest in him, but he had wanted nothing to do with them. His work had already made his life too complicated, and he didn't need anything else to make it more so. But even loyalty could go so far. The strain of being apart for years eventually took a toll on their marriage.

She asked for a divorce, and he willingly gave it to her.

He didn't harbor any ill feelings toward her. Whatever happened between them was his fault, not hers.

She had fulfilled her end of the bargain as his wife. She put him above everything else.

Before they met, Angie worked as a teaching assistant at a community college. Right after their wedding, she got an offer in another state for a full-time teaching position. It was around the same time Rhodes had found a position in the Newport Police Department.

She declined the offer. She much preferred to stay in a temp position than be away from her new husband.

Rhodes never realized the number of sacrifices she had made for him. Not having children was number one.

Rhodes stared at the empty glass. He thought about getting another drink, but two was enough. He couldn't afford to get drunk. He had a job to do.

Harold was facing life in prison, and Rhodes had the ability to do something about it.

No matter how hard it was for Rhodes to look Harold in the eye and not feel bitterness toward him, it must have been harder for Harold to ask for Rhodes's help. Rhodes was, after all, the man who was once married to his wife and had ultimately hurt her.

Rhodes took a deep breath. This was just another case, he told himself. It was no different from the dozens he had solved during his career.

But it wasn't, was it? What if Harold ended up in prison? Would Angie wait for Harold, or would she let Rhodes back into her life?

What about her children? Surely Rhodes could become a father figure to them. He never saw himself changing diapers, feeding babies, or even playing with them, but he could have a positive influence on her children. In fact, he might come to enjoy parenting.

Rhodes shook his head. He knew he was being selfish.

He didn't come here to destroy a family. He came here to restore one. His past was filled with sins, and this was his opportunity to atone for at least one. Angie deserved happiness, and if that was with her husband, Rhodes would do everything in his power to get to the truth.

He just hoped whatever he found was enough to save Harold Fulton.

SEVEN

Rhodes was about to leave the bar when he saw two police officers come through the front door. One of them approached the bartender and exchanged a few words. The bartender nodded in Rhodes's direction, and then both officers came over.

"Are you the new guy working on Harold Fulton's case?" the first one asked. He was skinny with dirty blonde hair, a crooked smile, and dark eyes.

Rhodes hesitated. He hadn't done anything wrong, so he wasn't sure why they were interested in him.

"I am," Rhodes slowly replied.

"I'm Officer Boyd Knepper," the man said, "and this here is my partner, Officer Steve Ainsley." Steve was much bigger, with broad shoulders, an army haircut, and when he smiled, there was a gap between his two front teeth.

Boyd took the seat across from Rhodes, and Steve pulled up a chair next to him. They had blocked off Rhodes's path to the exit.

"What's your name?" Boyd said, licking his lips.

"Martin."

"Full name?"

"Martin Rhodes."

"Well, Martin Rhodes," Boyd said, "I've never seen you in this town before. What are you doing here?"

"Helping out a friend."

"You mean Harold Fulton?"

32

"You can say that," Rhodes said. He then added, "Is there a problem, officers?" If there was, Rhodes didn't want to waste time with chit-chatting. Better they get it out right away. Rhodes had been in law enforcement long enough to know the methods officers used to extract information out of someone.

These two officers had started with generic questions to identify him, nothing a law-abiding citizen would have any concerns about answering. But then the questions would move on to more specific topics. That was when criminals slipped up. They would say something that would contradict what they had said earlier.

Rhodes wasn't going to take the bait.

Boyd frowned. "It's not really a problem. It's more like a nuisance."

Rhodes waited for him to elaborate.

"I see that you had put in a request to see my notes from the night of Kevin Williams's murder."

"I did. It was done through Mr. Fulton's lawyer, of course."

"Well, you see, I told Mr. Fulton's lawyer everything that happened that night. In fact, I believe he should have a copy of my statement in his file."

"He does, but I would like to read your official notes."

"Why?"

"In case we need to bring it before the court as evidence."

"You think I would lie about what happened?" Boyd looked over at his partner. "Is he calling me a liar?"

"I think he is," Steve said.

Rhodes leaned back and crossed his arms over his chest. He debated whether to get up and leave. There were witnesses in the bar, and unless he had done something wrong, he didn't have to answer any more of their questions. But Rhodes was new in town, and he didn't want any trouble. It was better he played along.

"I'm just trying to help Mr. Fulton," Rhodes slowly replied.

Boyd smiled. "Let me tell you something that you might not know: I wanna help him too."

Rhodes stared at him.

Boyd said, "I've known Harold Fulton for years. He's a good man. Kind, decent, educated. Runs a pharmacy. Follows the law. Got a nice family. Too bad about those robberies; they really shook him up. I told him sooner or later, the crooks would do something stupid and we'd be right there to nab them. But I guess he wanted to take the law into his own hands. He wanted his stuff back so badly that he went to that house with a loaded gun."

"He said he never took the gun with him," Rhodes replied.

Boyd shrugged. "I'm only telling you what we have as evidence. I'm sure you and his lawyer will come up with something to say otherwise, and that's your job, I get it. I just wished Mr. Fulton had called me before going to that house that night. Things might have turned out differently for him."

"Then I guess we both want the same thing," Rhodes said.

"And what is that?"

"To get to the truth."

Boyd looked at Rhodes and then nodded. "We do, don't we?" He stood up, and so did Steve. "What did you do before you came to Parish?"

Rhodes was waiting for that question. In a small town, everyone wanted to know your business.

"I was a detective," Rhodes replied.

"*Was*?"

"I'm no longer."

Boyd made a face. "Why not?"

"I killed a man."

Boyd shrugged. "We've all done that—in the line of duty."

"No. I shot him in cold blood."

Boyd's eyebrow shot up. "No shit."

"No shit."

"And you quit because of that?"

"I went to prison because of that."

Boyd smirked. "What's the point of having a badge when you can't even stay out of prison?"

Rhodes didn't know what to say.

"I'll have my notes sent to Mr. Fulton's lawyer," Boyd said. "I'll be seeing you around, *Detective* Martin Rhodes."

Boyd and Steve sauntered out of the bar.

Rhodes looked at his empty glass. His mouth was dry, but he was not in the mood for another drink.

He got up and left.

EIGHT

Rhodes stood outside the store with his hands in his coat pockets. Thick metal bars covered the front of the windows. They reminded him of the bars in his prison cell.

He pushed the memory away and examined the rest of the storefront. There was a "closed" sign on the door. The shop would remain closed until the owner returned or a new owner took possession of the business.

L&S Pharmacy was named after the previous owner, Larry, and his wife, Sandra. Together they ran the store for over forty years. Once Sandra passed away, Larry decided he didn't want to be in a place that reminded him so much of his wife. He chose to sell it, and who better to take over than his sole employee, Harold Fulton.

Rhodes knew this from his research on Harold. The more he knew about his client, the better he could serve him, he felt.

Rhodes wasn't even sure if he could call Harold a client, though. Rhodes wasn't being paid.

He had never been self-employed. In fact, he had been a detective for so long that he had stopped looking at his paychecks long ago. Every two weeks, the money was deposited into his account, and just as long as there was enough to pay the bills, he didn't care.

Now, things were different. He would have to keep track of all his spending—how much money came in, and how much went out. The problem was that Rhodes had little to no funds coming in.

"Sorry I'm late," Angie said as she walked up with keys in her hand. "The baby threw up right when I was leaving. I had to help my mother-in-law clean up before I left."

That was another reason why Rhodes didn't want any children. "That's okay," he said.

She unlocked the door, punched a code into the alarm keypad, and held the door for him.

He went in.

The pharmacy was narrow but long. There were shelves filled with all sorts of products, ranging from cold medications to basic toiletries to hygiene products.

Angie said, "You wouldn't believe how much you can make selling this stuff. People would come in to pick up their prescription and end up buying deodorant, toothpaste, even lip balm. The markup is excellent. It was why I always made sure to stock the store with as many products as possible."

Rhodes suddenly realized why he was not good with money. Angie was the one who was responsible for their budget. She made sure they didn't spend more than they made.

After ten years of staring at a six-by-eight-foot wall, a person could be forgiven for not remembering such things. How much money you had in your bank account or how good your credit scores were don't matter a great deal when you are in prison. There were other, more urgent things to be concerned about: whether someone was out to hurt you physically, or whether you were strong enough mentally to survive being locked up.

"Have you talked to your father yet?" Angie asked.

He stared at her but didn't reply.

"I know you two didn't get along, but after your sentencing, he sounded concerned about you."

Rhodes scoffed.

"He was worried that you might not make it out alive. Because, you know, you were a police officer."

"I did, and I'm fine. Tell me about the security," Rhodes said, wanting to change the subject.

"What do you want to know?" Angie said.

"How did the thief get in? I see iron bars on the window, I see a heavy lock on the door, and I see you have a security system. How could he get past all that?"

"That's a very good question. We thought we had taken all the necessary steps to prevent something like that from happening, but I guess we were wrong. According to the police, the thief cut the power line outside that led to our building. This disabled the security system."

"But wouldn't the security company realize something was wrong?"

"They did, and they quickly notified the police. When the police drove by, they thought it was a power outage. We've had some construction behind the building, and they figured a mistake made by a construction worker might have caused the power outage. The thief waited until the police were gone, and then he broke the glass next to the door and simply unlocked the bolt. He was in and out in a matter of minutes."

"But weren't there multiple robberies?" Rhodes asked.

"There were. The thief was brazen enough to do it the very next day. He figured no one would expect him to hit the same place twice."

Rhodes's brow furrowed. "Okay, but these robberies look sophisticated."

Angie gave him a puzzled look. "I don't understand."

"I mean, how can someone like Kevin Williams pull them off when he was an addict and homeless?"

"I thought the same thing," Angie replied. "The police believe it might have been more than one person. They think someone used Williams to pull it off. The police also believe this other person was the one who called Harold in the middle of the night."

"But why?" Rhodes asked.

"I don't know. Maybe they had a falling out with Williams and decided to give him up for extra money."

"But that doesn't make sense. Wouldn't Williams, in return, give his accomplice up?" Rhodes asked.

Angie shrugged. "I wish I knew all the answers. But you're the detective, Martin. You have to figure this out. I already have too much on my plate."

Rhodes nodded. He moved around the store. "Harold runs the pharmacy by himself?"

"No, he has an assistant. She comes in a few days a week. But after what happened, we had to shut the doors and let her go. We didn't know how long it would be until Harold went to trial, and we didn't have the money to keep paying her."

"Why not let her run the store?"

"She's still a student. Only Harold is licensed to dispense drugs in the state. He and I were hoping once she received her certificate, she could take on more responsibilities." Angie looked crestfallen. "Now, I'm not so sure what I'll do with the pharmacy."

"Do you have her address?" Rhodes asked. "I would like to talk to her."

NINE

Rhodes knocked on the door and waited. The apartment was located in a not-so-friendly part of town.

On his way there, he had two people approach him to find out if he was interested in buying marijuana or any other drug of his choice. He also had a group of young men eye him suspiciously when he entered the building. They must have thought he was an undercover cop. Rhodes couldn't blame them. He had his coat collar turned up, his hands were in his pockets, and he still had a cop's walk. Plus, he didn't look like he was afraid of punks. This meant either he was crazy and didn't care what happened to him, or he was police and he knew criminals would think twice before touching him.

Regardless, Rhodes was grateful the men did not impede his path. He wasn't sure how things would have turned out. The last thing he needed was to be arrested again.

He rapped his knuckles on the door once more.

"Who is it?" a female voice asked from inside.

"Christine Duncan?" Rhodes asked.

"Yes, who wants to know?"

He saw a shadow over the peephole.

"It's about Harold Fulton," Rhodes said. "Can I ask you a few questions?"

A few seconds later, the bolt was unlocked and Rhodes was staring at a tall, slim, attractive black woman.

"You're a lawyer?" she asked.

"Not quite, but I am working with Harold Fulton's family."

Just then, a neighbor opened her door and peeked at what was going on down the hall.

Christine said, "It might be better if we spoke inside."

She led Rhodes into the living room. Unlike the exterior of the building, the apartment was well-decorated and clean.

She noticed Rhodes staring at the furnishings and said, "We're only staying here so that we can save enough to buy a house."

"We?"

"My mom and I. Sometimes, my brother too, when he's not in jail."

"Is your mom home?" Rhodes preferred to keep their conversation private.

"No, she's a nurse and has night duty today. Can I get you anything to drink, Mister…?"

"Call me Martin. And no, thank you. I'm fine."

He sat on the soft couch, and she sat across from him.

"You're helping to get Mr. Fulton out of jail?" she asked.

"I'm trying to find out the truth."

"What would you like to know?"

"Angie—I mean, Mrs. Fulton—told me you were an assistant at the pharmacy."

"That's right. After passing the NAPLEX…"

"NAPLEX?" Rhodes was confused.

"The North American Pharmacist Licensure Examination. You need a bachelor's in pharmacy in order to take it, and after you've passed, you need to complete fifteen hundred hours of internship. That's why I was working at Mr. Fulton's place."

"How was Mr. Fulton as a boss?"

Christine broke down. Tears filled her eyes and she quickly reached for a box of tissues on the coffee table. After wiping her eyes, she said, "I'm sorry, but Mr. Fulton is a good man. I've learned so much from working with him. He's been so supportive of me getting my license. He'd give me time off whenever I needed to study. I'm just shocked by what has happened. He doesn't deserve to go through this. I pray for him every night. I pray for his wife and for his kids too. I pray for a miracle that they let him go."

"Where are you working now?" Rhodes wanted to move the questioning along.

"I'm not working right now," she quickly replied. "I can't—I refuse to believe what anyone says. Mr. Fulton is innocent."

"Why do you believe he's innocent?"

"He's a good man."

Rhodes was beginning to get tired of hearing that. It bothered him that the man who took his place was somehow better than him. Even if he was, shouldn't this mean Angie was in good hands? Rhodes had demons. His job as a detective required him to spend too much time dealing with the evil of society. Serial killers. Child molesters. Rapists. His obsession with catching those responsible for these horrible crimes made him a difficult man to deal with, let alone live with.

There were many nights when Rhodes would come home after working long hours on a case, and he would shut himself in a room in the basement. He would cut himself off from everyone around him, including his wife, so his thoughts could revolve solely around the crime and the person who had perpetrated it.

His obsession with getting justice for the victim overtook even his well-being. He would stop eating, and even his sleep would be affected. There were days when Rhodes would go about with not even an hour of sleep. Invariably, this would cause him to suffer severe headaches and even migraines.

The painkillers would help, but only for a short period. Once they wore off, the pain in his head came back full-force. He would feel like a fog had descended over his mind. He would be groggy and even irritable.

Rhodes never realized how his behavior must have affected Angie. Surely there were times she must have thought about leaving him. How can a person be with someone who detached themselves from everyone around them for long periods at a time? It must have been difficult and unfair, now that he thought about it. But she never once told him she was not happy. Maybe if she had, he might have corrected his ways.

But Rhodes had a sinking feeling he might not have.

He could be stubborn, which was an asset when solving a crime, but a liability when you had an argument with your spouse. He might not have appreciated all that she put up with and would have lashed out at her for being selfish. He would say he was serving society by bringing criminals to justice, and didn't she understand that?

In the end, though, it was *he* who was selfish.

Angie had married *him*, not his job.

"Are you okay?"

Christine's words jolted him out of his reverie. He blinked. "Sorry, you were saying Mr. Fulton was a good man."

"Yes, he wouldn't hurt a fly."

"But he would hurt Kevin Williams for the robberies at the store."

She laughed. Rhodes noted that she had perfect teeth. "Kevin was an addict, but he was not dangerous. There were many times he would come in and steal cold medication and even mouthwash."

"Mouthwash?"

"Yeah, for the alcohol in it. Kevin was never on hard drugs. He'd been on the streets for too long, and once in a while, he needed to get high, so he would come into the store. We knew why he was there, and more often than not, we would send him away empty-handed. Sometimes we would call the police, but only to deter him from stealing again. But he never threatened us, *ever*."

Rhodes listened intently.

"Even when we knew he had taken something, we never called the police on him," she continued. "We knew they'd put him in jail, and after a few months, he'd be back on the streets again. I think Mr. Fulton felt sorry for him. Many times, he would give him food and some money in the hope that Kevin would stay away from the medication. If you take too much of that stuff, you can do serious damage to your body."

"Okay, but then how do you explain the stolen merchandise from the pharmacy at the crack house?"

"I'm not sure, but I can tell you it wasn't Kevin who took that stuff. Whoever robbed the store went for the really expensive drugs we kept in the back. Some of those drugs can cost a couple of hundred dollars per bottle."

"If Williams wasn't a threat, then why did Mr. Fulton purchase a gun?"

"That I don't know. One day out of the blue, Mr. Fulton showed up with a weapon. I asked him about it, and all he said was that it was for our safety."

Rhodes nodded. He couldn't think of any more questions to ask her. He got up to leave.

Christine said, "Ever since Mr. Fulton went to jail, I've been keeping myself holed up in the apartment. You can stay and maybe tell me a little bit about yourself. It'd be nice to have someone to talk to."

Rhodes hesitated. He wasn't sure if he should tell her about his past. But something told him she wouldn't be shocked about his time in prison.

"I'm about to have dinner," she added. "You can join me, and if things go well, you can stay longer. My mom won't be back until morning."

Rhodes smiled. He liked the sound of that.

TEN

Rhodes was at a diner having breakfast, which consisted of eggs, sausages, tater tots, toast, and a cup of black coffee. It was more like brunch, but Rhodes had planned it that way. It allowed him to skip lunch. His funds were dwindling, and he had to think twice before going out to eat.

Christine had offered to make him breakfast early in the morning, but he wanted to leave her apartment before her mom returned. He preferred to avoid any awkward situations.

He knew sooner or later, he would have to consider some form of employment, but he wasn't sure yet what it would be. What did an ex-detective do with his life? Private eye work, perhaps? What about fraud investigation? Or even freelance consulting? It wasn't that Rhodes didn't want to work. It was more to do with who would hire him. He was a convicted murderer, after all.

Just then, he saw Boyd walk into the diner. Boyd looked around and came over to Rhodes after he had spotted him. He took the seat across from him.

"Kind of late for breakfast, isn't it?" Boyd said. He was not in uniform. He had on a two-piece striped suit instead.

The waitress came over. Boyd ordered plain coffee. He then pulled out an envelope from inside his suit jacket and slid it across to Rhodes. "You asked for it and I brought it. There are photocopies of all my notes from the incident at the crack house."

47

Rhodes pulled the envelope closer but didn't look inside. "I thought you were going to send it to Mr. Fulton's lawyer?" he asked.

"I was, but then I decided to bring it to you *personally*."

The waitress returned and placed a cup in front of Boyd. He watched her go and then said, "You see, I did some research on you. You were not lying when you said you spent time in prison. Hell, I thought you were making shit up to either impress or scare us. That takes a lot of balls what you did, throwing away your badge like that for 'justice.' I mean, either you are downright stupid or you've got some serious anger issues."

Rhodes stared at him. He knew Boyd was trying to get him riled up, but he wasn't going to give him the satisfaction. Boyd, however, was undeterred. He took a sip of his coffee and said, "During my research, I was surprised to find out that you were once married to Mrs. Fulton. It makes sense now why an ex-cop would come to a small town like Parish. It then raises the question, are you really here to help Harold Fulton or are you here to jeopardize his case? I mean, the man did steal your wife from you, after all. And he did it when he knew you couldn't do a lick about it. If I was in your position, I would want revenge. I would send that SOB to prison and take back what belonged to me. You know what I'm saying, right?" He gave Rhodes a crooked smile.

Rhodes was tempted to punch him in the face, but instead, he said, "How was the trial?" Rhodes tossed over a copy of the town's morning newspaper. He had read all about the case involving Boyd. The policeman had been charged with shooting a man in his car. Boyd had claimed he had pulled the man over for going through a red light. Boyd wanted to give him a ticket, but the man became enraged. During their argument, the man reached down in his seat, and fearing the man had a gun, Boyd had shot him. Later, a shotgun was found in the vehicle.

Boyd smiled. "Acquitted of all charges."

Rhodes understood why Boyd wasn't fazed when Rhodes had told him he had shot and killed a man. Just as long as there was probable cause, Boyd was fine with it.

"Your investigation come up with anything interesting?" Boyd asked.

"Nothing I can tell you."

Boyd leaned over. "I can help, you know. I know this town better than anyone."

"I'm sure you do," Rhodes said.

"If you got a suspect or a lead, I can go check it out for you."

Rhodes pushed his empty plate forward and straightened up. "I'll be fine. And you were the first officer at the crime scene, so your involvement can be constituted as a conflict of interest. Plus, there is something I wanted to ask you."

"What is that?"

"If Harold Fulton didn't call 9-1-1, how did you end up at the crack house?"

Boyd crossed his arms over his chest. "You really want to know?"

"I do."

"We got a tip. Someone had seen a white Buick drive away from the crack house in a hurry. The witness thought the driver was drunk and got the license plate number. I was close by, so I got the call to check it out. When I went to Harold Fulton's house, I didn't know that a murder had occurred. I found the Buick parked in the driveway. Out of habit, I flashed my light in the interior of the car. I was hoping to find liquor bottles, but instead, I saw blood on the driver's seat. I went inside the house and found Harold Fulton pale and terrified. I asked him about the blood. He said he didn't know how it got there, but after a bit of prodding, he confessed he had found a dead body in the crack house. I had no choice but to detain him until we knew what was going on. Later we discovered the body and corroborated that part of Fulton's story. We then searched his home and found the coat with the victim's blood on it, which we then matched to the blood found on the car seat. Also, we found the weapon that was used to shoot the victim in the glove compartment of his vehicle. It doesn't take a genius to see that Harold Fulton killed Kevin Williams."

Rhodes didn't say anything.

Boyd emptied his cup and stood up. "You got any more questions for me?"

"One more," Rhodes said.

"And what is that?" Boyd asked, annoyed.

"Who was the officer at the scene of the robberies?"

"I'm not sure."

"Can you find out and let me know?"

"Why is it important?" Boyd asked. He was champing at the bit to get on with his day.

"I just want to see the official report."

Boyd stared at him. "Fine," he said. "I'll see what I can do."

ELEVEN

The conversation with Boyd had left Rhodes feeling unsure of Harold's innocence. The more he dug into the case, the more he felt Harold might have committed the crime. There was motive and opportunity. Harold wanted his stolen merchandise back, and he found Kevin Williams in possession of it.

Rhodes took a deep breath. Why did he take on this case? he wondered. He should have excused himself the moment Angie had given him the facts. Boyd was correct. It didn't take a genius to put two and two together.

He hated to see Angie go through this again. She deserved all the happiness in the world. Maybe it was why he had taken on the case, so that he could give her back what she always wanted: a loving, happy family.

Rhodes was hoping Boyd would tell him something that might light a spark in his brain. It could be anything trivial—an offhand comment from a witness, seemingly insignificant evidence overlooked—something that could lead him in the direction he wanted to go: proving Harold's innocence.

Perhaps Rhodes needed to face the facts and stop his investigation. It was becoming an exercise in futility.

Rhodes stared at the envelope Boyd had just given him. He hated leaving any stones unturned.

He spent the next half hour going through Boyd's notes. They didn't contradict what Boyd had already told him.

Rhodes was ready to call it a day when he decided to give the file one more look.

Rhodes pulled out all the photos from the crime scene and laid them out on the table side-by-side. He grabbed the first one. It was a shot of the room at the crack house. It was small with a window on the left and a closet on the right. The room was littered with garbage and junk. In the middle was Williams's body.

Rhodes grabbed the second photo. It was a close-up of the body. Kevin Williams had on a black t-shirt, roughed-up baggy jeans, and dirty white runners with no socks on. He lay on his back with his eyes open. They were staring up at the ceiling. Rhodes could clearly see the bullet hole in the middle of his forehead. A pool of blood had gathered around the back of his head. This was exactly how Harold had described it.

Rhodes suddenly paused. He had seen this photo before, but now that he was staring at it again, there was something peculiar about the crime scene.

The wound in the forehead looked like it was committed by someone who was a good shot. According to Harold, he had never even held a gun prior to his recent purchase. Then how did someone with zero gun experience aim and fire a single shot directly between a man's eyes?

Maybe Williams was sleeping and Harold had surprised him, Rhodes thought.

Rhodes picked up the first photo again. There was no mattress in the room. That was odd. Perhaps Williams slept on the floor. He was, after all, homeless and an addict. He was already used to sleeping on concrete and cardboard boxes.

Rhodes then searched through the photos and grabbed another. It was a different angle of the room. Rhodes looked closely and saw no drug paraphernalia. No needles, no syringes, no smoke pipes, not even a single cigarette.

Why didn't I notice this before? he wondered. Maybe because it was a crack house, so he assumed there would be drugs.

Was Williams clean? If so, then why was he at the crack house to begin with?

Rhodes snatched up another photo. It was a shot of the boxes of medication found next to Kevin Williams's body.

A thought occurred to Rhodes. Why keep the medication out in the open? Why not hide them? Maybe even in the closet? The room didn't have a door. Surely, Williams knew the value of the medications. Why else would he steal them in the first place?

Rhodes examined the photo in detail. His mouth nearly dropped. He could clearly see that the seals on the medication boxes had not been tampered with. For an addict like Williams, his first instinct would have been to tear through the packaging and sample the contents inside. But he had not sampled a single item.

Rhodes began to get a nagging feeling that something wasn't right. No matter how long he'd been away from his job as a detective, some feelings never fully disappeared. They faded like a faraway memory, but they could be brought back with a little effort.

From the outset, this looked like an open-and-shut case. Harold was at the scene of the crime, and a gun that was registered to him was used to shoot the victim. Blood from the victim was also found on his person. A witness had seen Harold flee the scene. This caused the police to check on him, whereby incriminating evidence connecting him to the murder was found.

This raised more questions than answers. If Harold had shot and murdered Williams, why did he not dump the gun instead of leaving it in his glove compartment? Maybe he didn't have time to dispose of it? But then what about the blood on his coat? Why not wash it, or at the very least, trash the coat so that the crime wouldn't lead back to him? And then there was the matter of the medication. Harold's primary motive was to go to the crack house and retrieve the goods that were stolen from him. Why would he leave them behind instead of taking them with him?

Rhodes rubbed his temples.

There was more to this case then the obvious. This meant Rhodes's investigation was not complete. In fact, it was just beginning.

He gathered his belongings and left the diner.

TWELVE

Rhodes took a stroll through the streets of Parish. It was a working-class town where everyone knew their next-door neighbor. In his visits to bars, restaurants, and coffee shops, he overheard patrons gossip about Harold's case. It was a big deal for them. A respectable member of their community had committed a brutal crime.

Some believed Harold was innocent. They had known him for years and were willing to defend him at all costs. It was a setup, they argued. Someone wanted Harold out of the way, and they were willing to go to great lengths to get it done. They believed it was the big-box stores that were popping up in each town. These stores also provided pharmaceutical services. However, most of the locals—especially the seniors—preferred Harold over anyone else. They trusted him and thus were not willing to go to the competition. Now that Harold was in jail, they had no choice but to go elsewhere to get their prescriptions filled. Rhodes heard one elderly man vow that he would rather die than have some kid tell him what medication to put in his body.

Rhodes knew the supportive talk was all nonsense. The moment Harold was convicted for murder, the town would turn on him. They would start to spread disparaging gossip about him and his family. This worried Rhodes. He feared how the outcome of the case would affect Angie. She would probably have to leave Parish and start her life all over once again, but this time with two young children to care for.

When Rhodes had found out Angie was leaving Newport, the news had torn him up. Even though he couldn't be with her while he was in prison, just knowing she was not far from him provided comfort.

In many ways, it was better that she had left Newport behind. It allowed her to stay away from the city—and him.

The main streets of Parish were quiet at this time of the night. Rhodes preferred it that way.

He was still not used to his newfound freedom. When the judge had given him life with no chance of parole, he had resigned himself to the fact that he'd never walk the streets again. But then his sentence was cut short. The knowledge that one day he could go anywhere without having to look over his shoulder gave him renewed hope. And then, unexpectedly, he was told he would be set free.

There were only a handful of times when Rhodes had broken down in tears. One was when he found out his mother had passed away. Another was when he saw the distraught look on Angie's face during his sentencing. The most recent was when the parole board told him of their decision.

Rhodes had vowed that he would never go back to prison. And why should he? He was never involved in any illegal or criminal activity before. In fact, he was on the side of the law. How he ended up behind bars would not be repeated. It was why Rhodes refused to carry a gun: out of fear of what he would do with it. Even during the Franklin Strangler case, he went about unarmed. Plus, as a convicted felon, there was no way he could get a registered gun, and acquiring one on the black market was out of the question. Whatever he pursued next in his life, it would not involve weapons.

If law enforcement was out of the question, then perhaps a job in construction, he thought. He was big and strong, and he had sturdy hands, perfect for handling tools.

He stopped by the side of the road. He stared up at the clear sky. The moon was bright and full.

Rhodes couldn't imagine working at a construction site. He wasn't particularly good with tools either.

What about going back to school? he thought. He could get a diploma or certificate in something— *anything*. What that could be, he had no idea. Plus, Rhodes wasn't sure he wanted to spend the next couple of years of his life in a classroom.

Then there was the matter of money. He didn't have much, and he desperately needed to find a way to get some.

There were menial jobs out there that could solve his money problems. He could clean dishes at a restaurant, sweep floors as a janitor, or perhaps even drive a truck. But the only thing that ever excited him—and still did—was solving crimes.

This fascination had everything to do with his upbringing. He was surrounded by crime throughout his childhood, but it had the opposite effect on him. Instead of getting into trouble with the law, he had followed the law, which led him to the Newport Police Academy. He graduated at the top of his class. Within a few years of his graduation, he was promoted to detective.

If he hadn't gone to jail, he was certain he still would have been a detective.

He had no interest in becoming a sergeant or even the chief of police. All he longed for was arresting criminals. He just never imagined that one day he would end up being arrested.

His past had somehow caught up to his present. He grew up around crime, and now he was a criminal.

Rhodes looked at his watch. He decided to make a detour.

THIRTEEN

Rhodes knocked on the door and waited. Angie answered a few seconds later. "Martin, what are you doing here?"

"I wanted to ask you something."

"Um… can it wait? I'm getting supper ready for the children."

Just then, a boy appeared down the hall. He had dark curly hair and brown eyes, and he wore a shirt with a cartoon character on it. He came over and said, "Mommy, who is it?"

Angie looked at Rhodes and then at her son. "Um… this is…"

"My name is Martin," Rhodes said. He leaned down and held his hand out for him. "I'm friends with your mom."

The boy's small hand disappeared into Rhodes's big paw. "Like school friends?" the boy asked.

"Yes, you can say that," Rhodes said. Rhodes had first met Angie in high school. She was a cheerleader and he was on the varsity football team. They went out once but realized they didn't like each other. A few years later, they met again at a friend's party. He was in the police academy and she was studying social sciences. This time they hit it off.

The day Rhodes graduated from the academy was the day he proposed to her. Within three months, they were married and had even bought a house. They talked about children, but he kept putting the topic aside. She thought maybe it was too early in their marriage for them to have the discussion. One day he would change his mind and want his own, she believed, but before that day came, he was taken away in handcuffs.

"Are you going to join us for dinner?" the boy asked.

Rhodes looked over at Angie. She shrugged. "You can join us if you want."

Rhodes hesitated. He wasn't sure if it was a good idea. "Um… I actually have to…"

The boy said, "Mommy made macaroni and cheese with chicken nuggets. After that, we're going to have ice cream for dessert."

Rhodes paused, but when he saw the eagerness in the boy's face, he said, "I guess I can't say no to that."

The dinner had been far more enjoyable than Rhodes could've imagined. Angie's daughter was still a toddler, so she played with her meal more than she ate it. The boy, however, had a great appetite. He devoured each of his chicken nuggets, which he had covered with a thick layer of ketchup.

Afterward, Rhodes helped out with the dishes and then proceeded to the living room while Angie went upstairs to put the children to bed.

Rhodes walked over to the fireplace and grabbed a framed photo from the top of the mantle. It was of Harold, Angie, and the children. The photo was probably a couple of years old because their daughter was still a baby in the portrait.

"That was taken in Mexico," he heard Angie say from behind him. "Harold had just bought the pharmacy, and he took us to an all-inclusive resort to celebrate."

He nodded and put the frame back in its original position.

"Would you like some wine?" she asked. "I sometimes pour myself a glass after dinner. It helps calm me down before going to bed. Otherwise, I'll spend the night thinking about Harold and what he must be going through right now."

"Sure."

She returned with two glasses. She handed one to him and sat on the couch. "I'm sorry I didn't visit you in prison," she said.

He took a sip. "Even if you had come, I wouldn't have wanted you to see me like that."

She nodded. "I visit Harold every day in the county jail. I want to be there for him, you know. I want him to know that we—the children and I—are waiting for him at home."

"You've got a great family," he said. "They're good kids."

She smiled. "They're great." She then paused and looked at him. "Did you ever imagine us having a family?"

"Sometimes," he admitted, staring at the glass in his hand. "It was mostly at night in my cell when there was nothing but silence around me. That's when I wished for a lot of different things." He looked at her. "But you knew why I didn't want any children."

"I know, because of your dad. But you are not him."

"My father wasn't really there for me when I needed him, and I wasn't sure if I could be any different to my children."

"You would have made a great dad, you know," she said.

He shrugged. He did not believe her.

She said, "You know, I was mad at you for what you did to us… to me. I told myself that I could never forgive you. But when I had my son, I realized how hard it must have been for you to see that man, who you knew had killed a child, walk free. It must have eaten away at your soul. I witnessed the pain you were going through at that time, but I didn't know how to help you." She put her glass down. She leaned over and put her hand over his. "Children need protection, and no one protected that boy. You took it upon yourself to fix what was wrong. It is why I believe you would make a wonderful father because you would go through heaven and hell to protect your children."

He didn't say anything. He just stared at her hand.

She let go and lifted her glass once again. "So, what did you want to ask me earlier?" she said.

"Do you know where Harold kept his gun in the pharmacy?"

She thought about it. "I think I saw him put it underneath the cash register."

"Did he tell anyone else where he kept it?"

She frowned. "I don't know. *I* knew about it. I think Christine knew too."

"Can you give me the key to the pharmacy?" he asked. "I want to check it out one more time."

"What do you hope to find there?"

"I'm not sure, but something has been bothering me and I just want to confirm it."

FOURTEEN

Rhodes left Angie's house and decided to walk to his motel. It would take him twice as long, but he didn't care. It wasn't like he had someplace urgent to be at the moment.

It was the middle of the night, and the streets were empty. The walk would not only help process the wine through his system but also allow him to clear his head.

Dinner with Angie's family had brought back old feelings. The same feelings he had tried to suppress over the years. The moment he had found out that she had remarried, he had tried to forget her, but he could not. The divorce should have been the final nail in the coffin, but it was still not enough for him not to think that one day she might come back.

His sentence had been reduced to fifteen years once the truth had come out about the man he had shot and killed, which was a long time to wait for someone, but it was not forever. Angie would find it in her heart to take him back once he got out, he believed—wrongly perhaps—but it gave him comfort at a time when he needed it the most.

He knew it was over between them when she had moved to Parish with Harold. He had vowed not to think about her after that. She was an important part of his life before prison, but she would not be an important part after.

He had spent countless nights in his cold cell playing and replaying in his mind exactly what he would say to her once he got out. He was angry with her for abandoning him at his time of need. *Whatever happened to "for better or worse?"* he would silently yell while stuck inside his cell's four walls. But as quickly as the anger would come, it would dissipate. He didn't have the right to be cross with her. She didn't destroy their relationship. He did. He wasn't even sure if she ever wanted to see him again. *Why would she?* he thought. She had found another person to share her life with, and she had children to make her forget her life with *him*.

But life had an unexpected way of bringing people together. He was glad it did, although he wished the circumstances would have been different.

Being accused of murder was no laughing matter, and Rhodes wouldn't wish it on even his worst enemy. Harold was not his enemy. He had never harmed him. In fact, they had never been face-to-face until their recent meeting.

Rhodes knew Harold would not survive prison.

Years on the force dealing with the evilest criminals imaginable had made Rhodes hard. Harold was not. He was a mild-mannered pharmacist with a wife and two young children.

But all the evidence was pointing to him as the killer, and Rhodes was unsure how to figure it out.

Rhodes passed a shop's window and stopped. He stared at his reflection. Even in the low light, he could see the turmoil he was feeling. On one side were Angie and the kids, and on the other was Harold Fulton. Rhodes was in the middle. He felt like an imposter by just being there, but he wasn't the wedge between Angie and Harold; it was the impending sentence that Harold was facing.

Rhodes grimaced. Why did he feel like he had the power to change things? It wasn't like Harold's life was in his hands. It was the evidence against Harold that was the driving factor, not him. Rhodes was merely piecing a puzzle together.

He rubbed his face and took a deep breath.

Rhodes was never one to examine his feelings, but since his arrival in Parish, it was all he had been doing. Maybe it was for the best.

For ten years, he had bottled up his emotions. Ten years he had hid his true feelings from everyone. Who else could he share them with? The other inmates? The guards? The prison psychologist?

No.

He couldn't tell anyone because he couldn't show any sign of weakness. Prison was different than the outside world. The rules were not the same. If an enemy found your Achilles heel, they would not hesitate to use it against you.

Rhodes had kept his feelings coiled up inside him, and now he sensed they were ready to explode.

He took another deep breath. His nostrils flared as he sucked in cool air. His eyes were moist, but he would not allow himself to break down.

His entire body shook when he exhaled.

Rhodes would not force what happened next. Angie had already made her decision when she started a new family. Rhodes wished he could've persuaded her to reconsider, but quite frankly, it was none of his business. They were already divorced, and she could choose whomever she wanted to be with.

Harold's fate was not entwined with his.

Rhodes would leave Parish regardless of the case's outcome. There was nothing for him here.

FIFTEEN

Rhodes was a block away from his motel when he turned a corner and was promptly hit by a blinding light.

He instantly shielded his eyes with his forearm. He squinted and realized that it was coming from a car's headlights.

He focused his eyes and caught the silhouette of a man behind the wheel. The light was too strong for Rhodes to see who it was.

Rhodes debated whether to turn back and go around. But the longer the light hit him, the more irritable he became.

Someone was playing a game, and Rhodes was not in the mood for it. He would give the driver a piece of his mind.

Covering his eyes, he slowly moved forward.

A shadow loomed up behind him.

Before he could turn, something hit him hard across the back of the head—pain shot through his skull.

Rhodes fell forward but managed to break his fall with his hands. His ears were ringing and he felt disoriented.

He looked up, but the light blinded him again.

The shadow loomed over him.

The next thing he felt was a boot to his stomach.

He grimaced and balled his hands into fists. In prison, he had been jumped many times, and each time, he had inflicted more damage on his assailants than they had managed to inflict on him.

He vowed that this time would be no different.

Another boot came his way. Rhodes grabbed it in midair, held it for a second, but then he let go.

A second shadow fell over him, accompanied by a flurry of kicks and stomps all over Rhode's torso. He curled into a fetal position and let his attackers have their way. Fortunately for him, the assault didn't last long.

The shadows receded back.

Rhodes lifted his head up and watched as the attackers ran back to the car. The headlights faded as the car reversed and then disappeared from view.

Rhodes coughed and then stood up. He cleared his throat and spat on the ground.

There was no blood. *Amateurs*, he thought. But that didn't mean he wasn't hurt.

He looked around. The street was empty. There were no witnesses. And why should there be? It was the middle of the night, and most people were already asleep.

He ambled back to his motel.

He pulled off his coat and threw it on the bed as he headed straight for the bathroom.

In the mirror, he could see there was no major damage to his face, except for a slight cut on his lower lip.

He dabbed at the cut with a cloth soaked in cold water. He then tore off his shirt and examined his body. There were slight reddish marks just below his ribs. The bruising would turn purple, he knew, but nothing was broken.

Rhodes knew how painful broken ribs were. He had suffered through them during his stint in prison.

The beating he took tonight was nothing compared to what he had endured at the hands of other inmates. They were out for blood, and they would do anything to get you.

He once had an inmate attack him with a razor blade attached to the handle of a toothbrush. What made the attack more precarious was the fact that it was in the shower.

Rhodes's left arm and shoulder were cut badly during the altercation. Rhodes sacrificed his body because the attacker's main target was Rhodes's genital area. Earlier, the attacker had made sexual advances toward Rhodes. Rhodes had rebuffed them, and the inmate had decided to teach Rhodes a lesson in return. Fortunately for Rhodes, when the attacker was swiping the blade at his arm and shoulder, he slipped on a bar of soap. Seeing his opportunity, Rhodes went on the offensive. It took three inmates to pry him off his attacker, or else Rhodes would have killed him.

Rhodes went out and sat on the bed. From his duffel bag, he pulled out a bottle of painkillers. He downed a couple of pills with a half-empty bottle of beer and then lay in bed, staring up at the ceiling.

Whatever had just happened only reinforced what he was already feeling.

It was time to start putting the pieces together.

SIXTEEN

Rhodes searched the pharmacy but did not find what he was looking for. According to Angie, the thing he sought should have been underneath the cash register.

He looked around, and all he saw were shelves upon shelves of medication and other drugs.

He spotted a door in the back and immediately went there. The door was locked, but fortunately for him, he had a key.

He entered Harold's office and shut the door behind him. The office was small, and the furniture made it even more congested. There was a desk in the corner with a chair next to it. Several filing cabinets lined one side of the wall.

Rhodes sat on the chair and examined the top of the desk. There was a lot of paper. He sifted through them and found receipts, invoices, purchase orders, and various other documents. He grabbed a stack of opened envelopes. They were mostly bills.

Rhodes frowned. Harold may have been smart and educated, but he was not neat and organized.

He pulled open a filing cabinet and began sifting through the folders inside. Twenty minutes later, he shut the drawer and sat back.

Where could it be? he wondered.

It would be easier for him to go down to the county jail and ask Harold himself. But he wasn't sure the thing he was looking for would be of any help or not. The last thing he wanted was to give Harold false hope.

Rhodes knew a great deal about hope. Prior to his trial, his lawyer had indicated she might be able to work out a deal with the prosecution. Rhodes had an exemplary record as a detective, which she believed should amount to something in Rhodes's favor.

A deal was ready to be struck, whereby Rhodes would get fifteen years with a chance of parole after seven. But Rhodes's hopes were dashed at the eleventh hour when the prosecution retracted their offer. The lead prosecutor felt he had a strong enough case to put Rhodes away for life. He wanted to make an example of him. No person was above the law, he said.

Rhodes didn't feel betrayed. It wasn't like he was not guilty. He was. But like any human facing a hard journey ahead, he had hoped for some leniency. When he didn't get it, he accepted his fate and forged ahead. Harold, on the other hand, would be devastated if Rhodes's hunch did not play out. It was why he preferred to play his cards close to the chest.

At the moment, though, he had no cards to play with. Unless he found what he was looking for, his theory would stay just a theory.

Rhodes rummaged through more drawers, but again he came up empty-handed. He had a sinking feeling it was not here, even though it should be.

Maybe I should take another look at the shelf underneath the cash register, he thought. He might have missed something during his initial search.

Rhodes stood up.

It was then that he noticed it.

A corkboard was placed on the wall behind the desk. It was littered with tacked-on notes and various other pieces of paper.

He went closer and moved his eyes over the board. Above it were the words IMPORTANT & URGENT.

Harold had used it for stuff that required his immediate attention and that he felt was high-priority.

There was a reminder for a meeting from the local pharmacists club. There was a notice about an upcoming seminar from a large drug company. There were memorandums from the Food and Drug Administration. There was even a note from Angie reminding Harold of their visit to a prospective school for their son.

As Rhodes moved to the bottom of the board, he finally found what he sought. It was in the corner.

He extracted the piece of paper from the board and examined it. He couldn't help but smile.

He slipped the paper in his coat pocket and walked out of L&S Pharmacy.

SEVENTEEN

Rhodes stood at the corner of the intersection and watched as the cars stopped at the red light.

He looked up at the poles and didn't see any traffic cameras. He surveyed his surroundings and saw no retail shops nearby. This meant there were no cameras set by business owners either.

No cameras, no witnesses. A perfect location for a murder, he concluded.

There was, however, a coffee shop where the bus had dropped off Rhodes. But it was one traffic light away. Still too far to record or capture anything.

Rhodes was about to head back when a man appeared from behind the bush. He had a long, bushy beard, and his clothes were tattered and dirty. The man ran up to the intersection and began panhandling, approaching each vehicle to ask for money. Most drivers rolled up their windows and ignored him, but a few kinder souls pulled out some change and dropped it in his hat.

The man did this for almost twenty minutes. He was so focused on the task at hand that he did not notice Rhodes staring at him.

When the man was satisfied he had collected enough, he ran back and disappeared into the bush.

Rhodes followed him.

He was surprised to find a trail leading from the intersection to a tunnel below the road.

The man was about to enter it when Rhodes caught up to him. "Hey, mister."

The man stopped and turned. Before Rhodes could say another word, he bolted.

Rhodes was about to race after him when he noticed the silhouette of someone standing at the other end of the tunnel. Fearing this person would run away too, Rhodes said, "I'm not here to hurt you. I just want to ask you a few questions."

The silhouette did not move.

Rhodes shoved his hands in his pocket and pulled out a bill. "If you help me, I'll give you twenty dollars." It was more than Rhodes could afford, but he needed answers.

The silhouette hesitated.

"Please. Just a few questions, I promise."

He saw the silhouette move. A few steps later, a woman appeared from inside the tunnel.

She was young with bright green eyes. She wore a sweatshirt and cargo pants. She also wore a bandana, and Rhodes could see tattoos peeking out from under her sleeves.

"Show me the money," she said.

Rhodes held it for her and she snatched it from him. "What do you want to know?"

"Who was that man that ran away?"

"I don't know him. He just moved in a month ago. He's full-on crazy if you ask me. I think he was on hard drugs before. He's always talking to himself. He once tried to steal my stuff and I nearly hit him. Now he knows better to stay in his spot."

Rhodes realized the woman and the man had taken up positions at each end of the tunnel. This way, neither of them ran into each other.

"What about you? How long have you been here?" Rhodes asked.

She shrugged. "About a year, give or take. But I move around a lot."

"You have a family?"

"Who doesn't?"

"Then, why are you here?" Rhodes was curious because the woman didn't look like a drug addict. In fact, it looked like all her faculties were in order.

"I was in an abusive relationship. To get away from my boyfriend, I started sleeping on friends' couches. But my boyfriend would track me to wherever I was staying, so I found it was better to sleep on the streets where no one knew me. That was three years ago. But now I guess I'm just used to it."

"Why did you choose this place?"

"You probably saw the crazy guy panhandling at the intersection, right?"

Rhodes nodded.

"It's a good way to make money. But I don't panhandle. I clean windshields." She stood up straighter, a glint of pride in her eyes. "I prefer to earn my money, you know."

"You said you moved here about a year ago. Was there someone else living here when you moved?"

She nodded. "Yeah. There was another guy. He wasn't crazy, but he was an addict. I'd seen him drink bottles of detergent. But he was friendly, though. When he left, the crazy guy took his spot."

Rhodes pulled out a photo from his coat and held it out for her to see.

"Was this the guy?" he asked.

The woman looked at it and smiled. "Yeah, that's him. What happened to him?"

He was murdered, Rhodes wanted to say, but instead, he said, "Stay safe," and walked away.

EIGHTEEN

The nightclub was in a shady part of town. It was surrounded by a pawn shop, a motel, and a bar. It took Rhodes several minutes to even locate it. There was no sign out in front, and it was in a nondescript building.

The only way Rhodes could tell he was at the right location was the address. He had gotten it from the town's newspaper, and unless the reporter failed to get his facts right, Rhodes was confident this was it.

He banged on the metal door and waited.

There was a small window on the door. Rhodes was waiting for someone to peek out and ask for the password, just like in the days of Al Capone. Instead, he heard the unlocking of several bolts before the door opened slightly.

"What do you want?" a man said. His head was shaved, his stubble was gray, and he had a gold chain around his neck. His shirt was unbuttoned all the way to his navel, exposing graying chest hair.

"Are you the owner?" Rhodes asked.

"Who wants to know?"

Those four words revealed to Rhodes that the man was the owner. "I want to ask you a few questions."

"Not interested," the man replied.

He was about to slam the door shut when Rhodes kicked it with his heel. The door swung back, taking the man with it.

The man fell to the floor and yelled, "Bobby!"

A second later, another man appeared from inside the club. He was big, with tattoos on both of his arms and his neck. His hair was slicked back into a ponytail.

When he saw the owner on the floor, he growled at Rhodes and charged him.

Rhodes didn't move. When the man was inches away from him, Rhodes stuck his leg out. Bobby tripped, his face connecting with Rhodes's knee as he dropped to the floor, landing next to the owner. He clutched his face. Rhodes could see blood welling up between Bobby's fingers.

"You broke his nose," the owner said.

Rhodes leaned down and lifted the owner up by his collar. "If you don't answer my questions, I'll break something of yours."

Fear blazed in the man's eyes. "Okay, okay, take it easy. Don't hurt me."

Bobby was whimpering. Rhodes said, "Tell him to put some ice on it."

"Listen to the man," the owner ordered.

Bobby quickly got on his feet and ran away.

"What do you want?" the owner said.

"What's your name?" Rhodes asked.

"Corbin, but people call me Corby."

Rhodes released him and said, "Corby, how long have you owned this place?"

"Not even six months."

"What happened to the previous owner?" Rhodes knew the answer, but he wanted to confirm it.

"I don't know."

"Sure, you do. It was in the morning papers."

"I do, but if you already know, then why are you asking me?"

"Did you have anything to do with his death?"

"What? Are you crazy? I was friends with the guy. He even let me manage the club when he was not around."

"So how come it's yours now?" Rhodes asked.

"After what happened to him, his wife didn't know how to run the place, so she put it up for sale. I figured I should invest in my future, so I bought the place. I didn't have the money, but she's letting me pay her in installments. Did she send you to collect? I don't pay till the first of the month, you know."

"No, she didn't send me."

Rhodes put his hand in his pocket. Corby jerked back and held his hands up to shield himself.

"Don't worry, I'm not going to hurt you," Rhodes said. He pulled out a piece of paper and then unfolded it. It was the front page of yesterday's newspaper. "Did this man ever come to the club?"

Corby hesitantly moved forward and squinted. "I think I saw him a couple of times."

"Did you ever see him talk to the previous owner?"

Corby shrugged. "I couldn't tell you for sure. It's usually so busy here that I can't keep track of who's talking to whom."

"Did the guy ever come in here in an official capacity?" Rhodes asked.

"You mean to raid the place?"

"Yes, for drugs and narcotics."

Corby shook his head. "We don't allow drugs in the club."

Of course that's what he would say, Rhodes thought. But he knew from past experience that places like these were heavily involved in illegal activities.

A deal had gone bad, and this had caused the previous owner to end up dead. Rhodes was certain of it now.

He had connected the dots, and he knew who the real killer was. He had been suspicious from the beginning, but it was not until his back was to the wall that he became more focused. Now it was time to end this.

Rhodes's thoughts were interrupted when he heard Corby say, "What are you going to do to me?" His eyes were fixed on Rhodes's hands. Rhodes didn't realize they were balled up in fists.

Rhodes had always been able to use his height and weight to his advantage. He could be intimidating when he wanted to be, and he had a mean streak in him. He tried to suppress it as best as he could, but sooner or later, it always came out. He blamed his father for it. He brought out the worst in Rhodes, and he hated him for it.

He wondered if it was his childhood that made him end up in prison in the first place. But it was also his childhood that made him survive it.

It reminded him of the saying, "You can take the boy out of the gutter, but you can't take the gutter out of the boy."

Rhodes had tried to wash away the sins of his past, but the sins had come back to haunt him.

He stared at Corby for a second and then left the nightclub without saying another word.

NINETEEN

The sun had begun to set as Rhodes took a sip from his soft drink. The bar was full. There was a football game playing on the giant TV screen. A group of young men was already gathered around it. They were dressed in their team's uniform. Some had even gone as far as to paint their faces with their team's colors. They were getting louder with each drink they consumed, fired up on alcohol and the luck their team was having, but the bartender did not look concerned. They were buying drinks, and that's what mattered to him.

Rhodes was on the opposite end of the bar, far away from them.

They were enjoying their game, and he was enjoying his drink. Rhodes had had a particularly busy day.

Earlier, he had visited the county jail. He had a long talk with Harold. There were some things he needed clarification on. Rhodes could see that the stress was taking a toll on Angie's husband. He looked even frailer than during his first visit. He was clearly falling apart already. It wouldn't be too long before he had a serious health crisis.

Rhodes couldn't divulge the reasons for his visit. He feared Harold might blurt it to someone—a guard perhaps.

No, Rhodes had to tread carefully. The town was small enough for news to spread like wildfire. If that happened, his plan would not work.

His next visit was to Angie's house. Angie was on her way to her mother-in-law's house. She had to pick up the children. Rhodes requested five minutes of her time, which turned into an hour. He wanted to tell her something, and she was more than eager to hear it.

His last stop was at the police station. Afterward, he came straight to the bar. He had been there a good two hours by that time.

Rhodes's glass was almost empty. He knew soon enough the bartender would approach him for a top-up. Rhodes had already downed three glasses, and he wasn't sure if he could manage any more. The soft drink was starting to bloat his stomach.

He couldn't afford any problems, at least not that night. He had to be sharp and focused on what he was about to do next. He wasn't even sure if it would work, but he could see no other choice. A man's life depended on Rhodes's gamble.

Normally, when Rhodes was at the end of a case, he was running on pure adrenaline. He had cracked the case and was then heading for the finish line.

He didn't feel any rush that night. It was more trepidation than anything else. A lot could go wrong.

Rhodes glanced up at the clock.

It was time.

He put the glass down and headed to the back of the bar. Next to the men's restroom was a pay phone. He stuck a coin in and dialed a number. "This is Martin Rhodes. I've got some news for you. I know who killed Kevin Williams."

TWENTY

Rhodes stood in the room and stared at the spot where a dead body once was.

The crack house was vacant, but it had more to do with the police tape on the front door than any addict steering clear of the place because of a murder.

Rhodes shouldn't be here either. He knew full well he had broken the law by entering a crime scene, but he did not care. After tonight, the police would have bigger things to worry about than him.

A light flickered outside the window, followed by the sound of a vehicle coming to a stop.

Rhodes left the room and went downstairs.

He heard footsteps on the front porch. He watched as the front door handle turned.

Rhodes moved back away from the door.

The door swung open. It was Boyd Knepper. He was dressed in his uniform. "You're not allowed to be inside," he said once he saw Rhodes.

"It was getting a bit chilly out there."

Boyd looked around. "This place is a shithole and it stinks in here. Why couldn't we have talked at the diner, or anywhere else for that matter?"

"It might be better if we discussed things here."

Boyd put his hands on his belt. "Okay, so tell me who killed Kevin Williams? Isn't that why you called me here?"

"I think you already know."

"Yeah, it was Harold Fulton."

"We both know it wasn't."

"So, who was it?"

"*You.*"

"Are you kidding me?" Boyd was incredulous. "You brought me all the way here to accuse me of shooting some bum?"

Rhodes didn't reply.

"I should arrest you for breaking and entering, you know," Boyd said, pointing a finger at Rhodes. "Do you have any new evidence to back this accusation up?"

"I do."

"And are you going to tell me, or do you want me to guess?"

"It was something you had said that triggered it for me. You told me that a witness had called in about a drunk driver. And when you went to check it out, you found the blood in Harold Fulton's car."

"Yes, that's right. I was in the area and I went to investigate it."

"The thing is, if you were close to Harold's house when the witness had called, you should have been at the house *before* Harold reached it. The drive from the crack house to Harold's house is over an hour."

Boyd stared at him. "So? That still doesn't prove anything."

"True. But then it got me thinking about the robberies at the pharmacy. The crime was sophisticated, and Kevin Williams was not. He was homeless and an addict. There was no possible way for him to know how to cut the power to the building. But you would."

"What possible reason would I have to rob a pharmacy?" Boyd said through clenched teeth.

"You had two reasons. One: to frame Williams so that Harold Fulton would go after him. Two: to steal the gun Harold kept at the pharmacy in order to use it to shoot Williams."

"You have no proof of this," Boyd replied.

"Actually, I do." Rhodes pulled out a piece of paper from his coat pocket. He held it up for Boyd. "It's the gun permit I took from Harold's office. The officer who authorized it was you."

Boyd's face darkened.

"I visited Harold in the county jail today, and he confirmed that after the robberies, it was *you* who had encouraged him to get a weapon. He also confirmed that he told you where he kept it secured in his pharmacy." Rhodes paused to let his words sink in. "Then, when I asked you about the officer who was first at the scene of the robberies, you attacked me."

"You are lying," Boyd replied.

"I wish I was. It was you that night who kicked and stomped me. I was ready to defend myself when I caught your boot. They are the same boots you are wearing now. I would know. I used to be an officer before I became a detective. You hoped the attack would stop me from continuing my investigation. But you made a big mistake. It only further confirmed my suspicions, and it made me want to keep going even more."

Boyd said, "Why would I do all that, huh? Why would I go through all that trouble?"

"You did it to silence Williams."

Boyd scoffed. "I had never seen him before."

"You saw him when you shot the owner of the nightclub."

Boyd turned pale.

"I went to the nightclub and I showed your photo to the new owner. He confirmed that he had seen you there before. I believe you and the previous owner had a deal that had soured. I don't know the details, but they are not important. What is important is that you pulled over the nightclub owner one night and you shot him. You then planted the shotgun on his person. What you didn't realize was that Kevin Williams panhandled at that very intersection. He had witnessed the shooting. You couldn't shoot him too. How would you explain two deaths by your hand? You had to come up with a plan. You were aware that Williams had taken merchandise from the pharmacy before. Parish is a small town, so news spreads fast. This gave you a perfect opportunity to get rid of him."

Boyd glared at Rhodes.

"You broke into the pharmacy and stole the gun and merchandise to make it look like a robbery," Rhodes continued. "You then used Harold's gun to shoot Williams and staged his body at the crack house. You knew the place was vacant, having visited it before during your patrols. You subsequently called Harold and instructed him to come to the crack house to retrieve his goods. While Harold was inside the house, you planted the weapon in his glove compartment and covered his seat with Williams's blood."

Boyd was silent.

"You watched from a distance as Harold came running out of the house, got in his car, and drove away. You knew he would be in too much shock to notice the blood on the seat. This would place the victim's DNA on his clothing, thus further reaffirming that he was guilty of the murder."

Boyd said, "He could have called the police when he found the body. Why didn't he?"

"Even if he did, you already had a plan in place. You would leave the weapon on the property, and when you or someone else showed up, they would be able to match the bullet found in Williams's body to the gun registered to Harold." Rhodes crossed his arms over his chest. "I have to give it to you. You thought of everything. The picture you painted was perfect. But you made one big mistake."

Boyd frowned. "And what is that?"

"You didn't think someone like me would show up and start seeing the cracks in your perfect painting."

Boyd stared at him. "If you expect me to confess, you are wasting your time. You have no evidence. What you have is a theory. And quite frankly, no one will believe an ex-con like you."

Rhodes nodded. "I fully expect that. But whatever I've told you, I will also pass on to the people at Matheson, Rosenthal and Geltoff. I'm sure when they start digging into my *theory*, they will quickly start seeing the holes in your story. *You* had a problem with the owner of the nightclub. *You* shot and killed him, even though right now, you have been acquitted of the crime. *You* encouraged Harold Fulton to get a weapon, even though he had never fired a gun in his life. *You* were the one who showed up at Harold's house on the night of the murder. *You* were also the officer at the scene of the robberies. Your notes will prove this. Plus, I'm confident that there was no call to the police about a drunk driver. If a witness had made the call, you would not have been the officer at Harold's house. You were an hour away at the crack house, framing him for murder. Once Harold's lawyers get their hands on my investigation, I guarantee their focus will turn on *you*."

Boyd's left eye twitched. He blinked.

He pulled out his gun and aimed it at Rhodes.

Rhodes did not move. "You're not going to shoot me."

"Why not?" Boyd said. "I'll say it was self-defense. It worked once. Why wouldn't it work again?"

"If you shoot me, you'll have to shoot a witness too."

"What witness?" Boyd said.

"You can come out now," Rhodes said.

Someone appeared from the shadows. It was Angie. She had a look of pure disgust on her face. "We trusted you," she said. "You were supposed to protect us. You framed my husband."

Boyd turned his gun on her. She stiffened.

89

"You'll shoot us both?" Rhodes said. "How will you explain that?"

"I'll say you shot her."

"With whose gun? Yours?"

Boyd was confused.

Rhodes said, "The last time, you were able to plan out all the details. This time you can't."

"No one will believe you," Boyd growled. "Especially not a convicted murderer and the wife of a man soon to be convicted of murder."

"But I believe them," a voice said from behind them.

TWENTY-ONE

Boyd turned and found Officer Steve Ainsley standing by the door.

Boyd blinked. "What are you doing here?"

"He asked me to come." Steve nodded in Rhodes's direction. "It took a lot of guts for him to come and see me, even though he knew I was with you that night we roughed him up." Steve turned to Rhodes. "I'm sorry. I didn't know the whole story. I thought you were in Parish to cause trouble. It was only meant to scare you away." Steve faced Boyd again. "What you told me were all lies."

"Don't listen to them," Boyd said. "They're trying to confuse you."

"No, they're not. I heard everything."

Boyd blinked again. "You're not going to take their side, are you? I'm your partner, Steve."

"It was why I went along with everything you did, Boyd. You told me the story about the nightclub owner, and I believed you. That's what partners do. They are honest with one another, and they have each other's back. I knew you skirted around the law, and as your partner, I accepted that. I just never thought you were a murderer. And to make matters worse, you tried to frame an innocent man." Steve's voice turned hard. "Boyd, put your gun down. I'm arresting you for the…"

A shot rang out. Steve didn't have time to react. A bullet ripped through his shoulder. He fell to the floor like a rag doll.

Boyd turned the gun on Rhodes and Angie, but Rhodes had already charged him with his shoulder down. Rhodes was bigger and stronger, and when he hit Boyd, the impact knocked him ten feet back.

The gun flew out of Boyd's hand and hit the wall.

Before Boyd could recover, Rhodes jumped on his chest, pinning his arms with his knees. He then pounded Boyd across the face with his big fists. He continued until the killer's nose, cheeks, and mouth were covered in red. He only stopped when Boyd let out a weak groan.

Rhodes stood up and looked over at Angie. He was expecting her to be horrified by what she had seen. Instead, she had a look of satisfaction on her face.

She came over and hugged him.

It felt nice to once again feel her warmth. He had dreamed of this moment for years. He had longed to touch her, feel her next to him, and hold her. But he knew things were different now. She was only embracing him because he had exonerated her husband.

Regardless of the circumstances, he put his arms around her and held her close one last time.

TWENTY-TWO

Rhodes watched through the kitchen window as Harold played with his son and daughter in the backyard.

Steve Ainsley had survived the shot to his shoulder, and with his testimony, Boyd Knepper was given fifty years for the murder of Kevin Williams and the owner of the nightclub.

Harold was released immediately. The pharmacy was open once again with Christine Duncan, his assistant, taking over more of the duties. Harold had decided he would work less and spend more time with his family. They were the most important thing in his life, after all.

As Harold laughed with his children, Rhodes felt a tinge of regret. He almost wished he could switch places with Harold. But wishing could not change reality. He knew this home and this life was not his reality.

"Are you sure you can't stay?" Angie asked. Rhodes faced her. "I don't belong here."

"I didn't think I did either, but with Harold and the kids, its home now."

He nodded.

She walked up to him and put her hand on his cheek. "Thank you," she said. He stared at her. "Thank you for giving me my husband back."

He placed his hand over hers.

The back door slid open. "Sorry," Harold said. "Am I interrupting something?"

"No." Angie pulled away from Rhodes. "We were just talking."

Harold said, "Angela told me you are leaving."

"My job is done here." Rhodes grabbed his duffel bag and walked to the front door.

"Where will you go?" Angie said.

"I heard Bridgeton is a nice place to settle down. Hopefully, I'll find something to do there."

Harold held out his hand. "Thank you, Mr. Rhodes."

Rhodes shook it. "Call me Martin."

Harold pulled out an envelope and placed it in Rhodes's hand. "What is this?" Rhodes asked.

"A token of my appreciation," Harold replied.

Rhodes could tell there were a couple of thousand dollars in the envelope. "This is really not necessary. I…"

"Please, take it," Harold insisted. "Without you, I would be rotting in jail right now. I owe you far more than this. I owe you my life, Martin." His eyes glowed with sincerity.

Rhodes nodded and slipped the envelope into his coat pocket.

He waved goodbye and made his way down the driveway.

They watched as he walked down the street and then disappeared from view.

Angie and Harold held each other tight. They were grateful that Detective Martin Rhodes had come and saved their family.

Visit the author's website:
www.finchambooks.com

Contact:
finchambooks@gmail.com

Join my Facebook page:
https://www.facebook.com/finchambooks/

MARTIN RHODES

1) Close Your Eyes
2) Cross Your Heart
3) Say Your Prayers
4) Fear Your Enemy

THOMAS FINCHAM holds a graduate degree in Economics. His travels throughout the world have given him an appreciation for other cultures and beliefs. He has lived in Africa, Asia, and North America. An avid reader of mysteries and thrillers, he decided to give writing a try. Several novels later, he can honestly say he has found his calling. He is married and lives in a hundred-year-old house. He is the author of the Lee Callaway Series, the Echo Rose Series, the Martin Rhodes Series, and the Hyder Ali Series.

Made in the USA
Monee, IL
29 September 2024

66797176R00056